Di

This is a satirical work. I am poking fu... ...
utmost respect. I don't mean to offend anyone, I'm mainly making fun of myself for poetry that I have written that I consider cringe worthy. If you feel personally attacked by any of these jokes I'm sorry that you're bad at writing. (That's a joke, too. I am truly sorry if I offend anyone.)

$1 of every book sold will go towards WAVAW Rape Crisis Center in support of victims of sexual assault. For more information, visit WAVAW.ca
Thank you for your support.

Love you.

before we begin.
I know half these jokes are about winter and snow and aren't relevant anymore
But is your book more relevant than mine?

Is it, Jackie?

Oh that's right.

    You didn't write a book.

Hop off my dick.

<u>carnivore.</u>
I wanted to be with you
but I was indica
and you, sativa

and you didn't like
salads

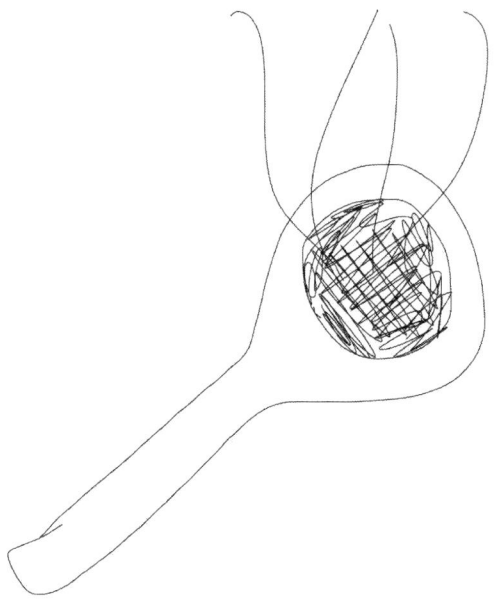

unbrofessional.
/ənbrəeSH(ə)n(ə)l/

adjective

below or contrary to the standards expected in a particular brolationship
    "a report on unbrofessional conduct"
being a bad bro
    "chad fucked my girl"
    "damn that's unbrofessional"

<u>nauseous.</u>
I drank you like a 12 pack
of Mikes Hard

And just the same;
the hangover wasn't easy

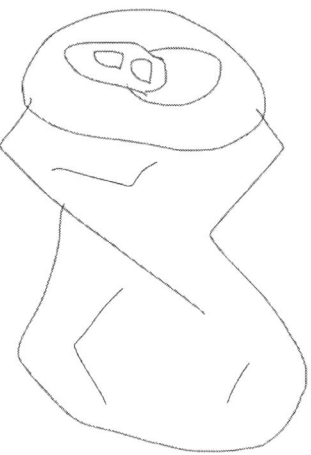

<u>scientific fact.</u>
You are made of stardust
that's probably why
you already feel dead

Because technically you are

tumblr.
i don't sleep
cigarettes
razorblades
coffee, black
vinyl and
      cigarettes

Cringe past writing 1: original edge (14)

I guess in simple
she's the sun and I'm the moon
she lives in a time of wonder and opportunities
while I hang low in late night regrets:
lost lovers and broken hearts

the world wakes at her gleam;
taunting it with new possibilities

while I am the time of the forgotten
vodka comas, black out friday's
and the sadness of 2 am

she is the sun and I'm the moon
she is for the hopeful
I am for the damned

<u>justice.</u>
I worked so hard
too give myself the life I've always wanted
and now I'm here:
in bed until noon
high
and watching youtube videos

Well deserved.

small town fairytale.
they were romeo and juliet
except he was a cop
and she was a nurse
so instead of killing themselves
they abused their power
and were racist

that's supposed to be a police badge & a stethoscope

<u>vine reference.</u>
yo
did we ever find out
why zack was kicking his leg
and refused to stop

where is he now

<u>please don't call me out i'm already so insecure.</u>
i just found out
there's girl call out groups
on facebook
and now girls
are scary to me again

<u>fuckboy.</u>
chad
      dylan
brad
      duncan
zack

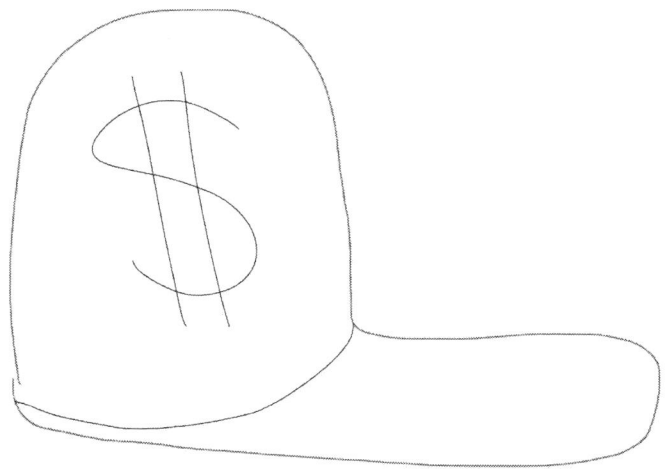

Cynical
Incinerate
Gasoline
Asphyxiate
Rectify
Enigma
Toxicity
Tainted
Exodus

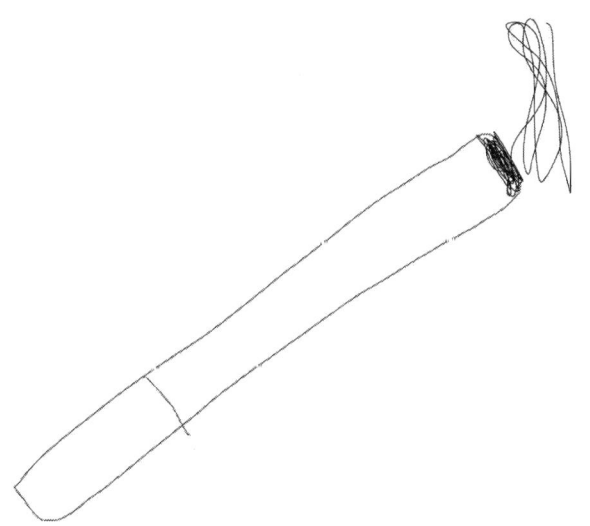

<u>broke.</u>
we drank cheap spirits
and smoked cheap cigarettes
and had cheap sex

we said it was all for aesthetic
but really, we were just poor

<u>high.</u>
I thought you were an angel
glowing in the dark
but really
I had just taken too many vicodin
and I was real fucked up

<u>friends? maybe. hard to say.</u>
"eyebrows are sisters not twins" I cry
while mine are clearly not even blood related

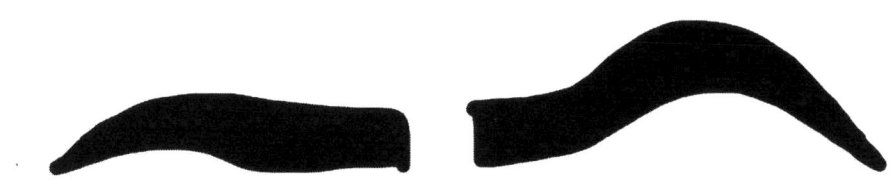

<u>stinging.</u>
nothing stung more
than the burn
of your rejection
except maybe
the other burn you gave me
yknow
the one i needed that cream for

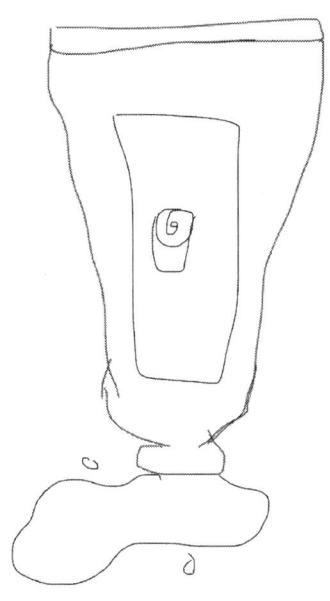

<u>infantile.</u>
I still get my mom
to check my shoes for spiders

This isn't really a poem
I just think it's cute

<u>gotcha.</u>
so to be clear
you aren't ready for a relationship
and just want to continue
doing what we've been doing

which is
seeing each other 3-5 days a week
meeting each others friends
and families
having sleepovers
having sex
and saying i love you

mix-up.
I asked for coke
you gave me pepsi
I meant the drug
you didn't even try

<u>unprepared.</u>
you were a winter blizzard
and I was a set of summer tires

<u>pants on fire.</u>
whisper whisper
in my ear
tell me lies
that hope is near
patronize
my little heart
your way with words
is an art

Cringe past writing 2:issues with friends (13)
This is once
Twice
Three times too many
Forgiveness is gone
You've hurt me plenty

It took me some time
But I now realise
I've come back
One
Twice
Three time too many

Hello and goodbbye
Baby welcome to real life
It's the place you left
Once
Twice
Three times too many

The past, exquisite
A timeline I'd want to visit
Although I know
Once
Twice
Three times are plenty

Numbers add on
From the days that I have seen you
My sadness lingers on
And it's time to say
"Bonjour mon dernier au revoir"
Because,
Once
Twice
50 times is too many.

<u>Tumblr. 2.0</u>
broken glass
blood red
contrast
dead eyes
worn mask
fake smile and
       cigarettes

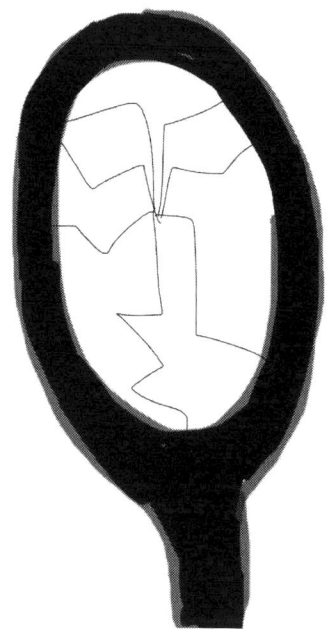

<u>ur not my dad.</u>
you asked me to call you "daddy"
and I'd be your little girl

but we weren't even blood related

so idk how that lineage would work

opposites.
you learned to dance
by twerking
in your bedroom mirror

I learned by playing
dance dance revolution

we are not the same

nope.
bitter bitter
cold and wither
I refuse to exist
in this weather
bring me rain
or bring me clouds
but ill fucking kill myself
if one more flake falls down

<u>my counsellor was right.</u>
even when i masturbate
i get off to the thought
of giving pleasure

so even in my wildest fantasies
i'm focused on someone else's happiness
over mine

<u>the only boy I've ever truly loved.</u>
one time
when I was sad
a boy said to me
"don't bake up a batch of frownies"
I don't think he knew
that would give him
a brownie point
in my heart

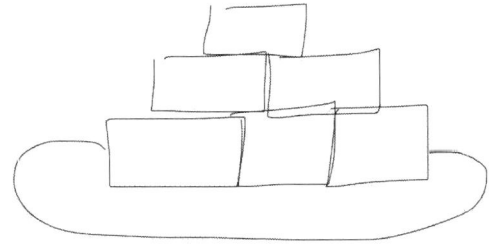

<u>nerd.</u>
yeah
you're cool now
   maybe
but i haven't forgotten
when you were
a soccer kid

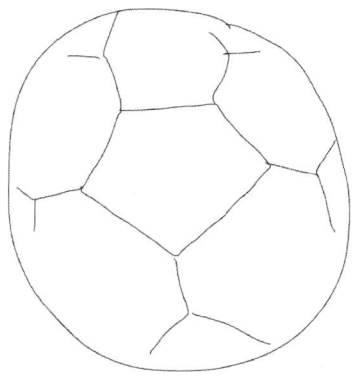

<u>i know you sent me to voicemail.</u>
You called me a psychopath and bitch you don't even have a fucking clue. You think you know me but you don't know half the twisted, cynical thoughts I think and plot, daily. So watch yourself, boy. Because I will learn every little detail about your life. And then I will ruin it. Slowly and methodically. Piece by piece. Until you forget what it feels like to live a life worth living. Or even worth enduring. Until you have nothing. Because you are nothing.

Okay, love you baby, call me back!

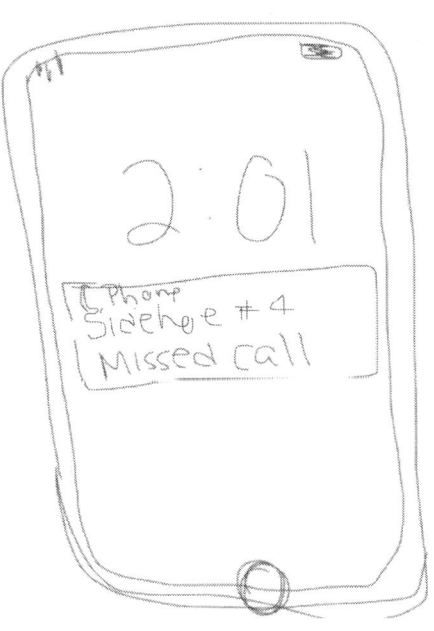

<u>addict.</u>
i think I'm overdosing
on the H
of your heart

<u>respect.</u>
For a while guys kept sending me
unsolicited dick pics on twitter,
so as a joke,
and as revenge,
I decided to rate the dicks I received
and tweet the ratings with the guys' @'s

After I did a couple, someone followed me,
liked the tweets I made making fun of other mens small dicks,
and then proceeded to send me a picture of their penis
next to a bic lighter
just to prove
 just how small it is

I wasn't even mad
Power move

Rating: 10/10

Tasty
Apathy
Rancid

<u>coping.</u>
Mental illness is weird

I just laid on my bathroom floor
for two hours
in complete silence
contemplating suicide

before deciding

"Ok time to masturbate"

I don't not appreciate it, though.
"Oh my god!
You look so thin!"

                        Yes thank you
                        It's the eating disorder

<u>Tumblr 3.0</u>
tragically beautiful
manic pixie dreams
smoking in my room
polaroids
ripped tights, leather jacket
      cigarettes

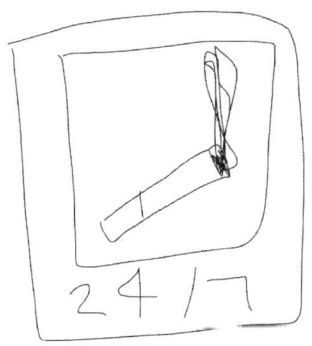

<u>braindead.</u>
You're cyclical like the weather
repeating the same patterns
and yet, somehow
just like the dumb bitches
who don't change
from their summer tires

I'm always surprised
when it snows

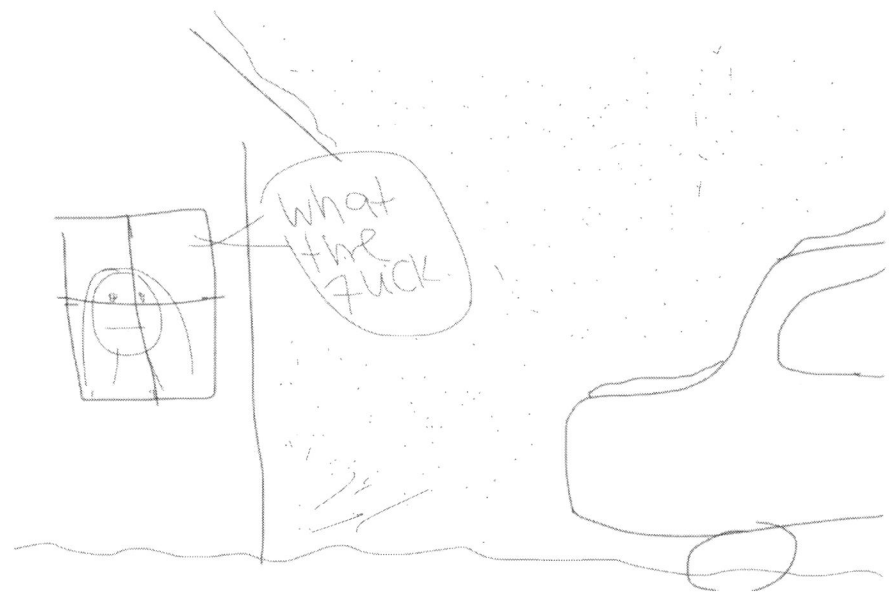

<u>slurp.</u>
i swallowed a parasite
when you made me swallow my feelings
and it's been eating me alive
ever since

Cringe past writing 3: crippling expectations (13)
A misty shadow
From above the grave
To forever enter her destiny
Of a slave

A slave of acceptance
Forgiveness
and hope
A place she may reach
The top of the steep slope

The waking twilight
From beyond her gaze
And there begins her future
All but a haze

Hazy dreams
and hazy lies
To fall the beginning of a battle
In which no body can survive

The dawn falls,
slowly rises
In which she despises
Her faith slowly following
for weeks upon days.

<u>recommendation.</u>
@ the bitch
that hates me
but still stalks
my shit:
          listen to grace kelly
          by mika
   love you

<u>self love.</u>
I've been looking
for my sad skinny white boy
with long hair
but maybe I'M
the sad skinny white boy with long hair

<u>crash.</u>
you were black ice
and i was speeding

<u>blue lips.</u>
once a month
i jump into the lake
no matter how cold it is
it makes me feel alive
i have the same approach
with love

PDA.
Here's your friendly
mom lecture
to remind you
that it's not lame
to get yourself checked
for STI's

Actually, it's rad
as heck

Self care type shit

Pee in a cup
and give the stigma up

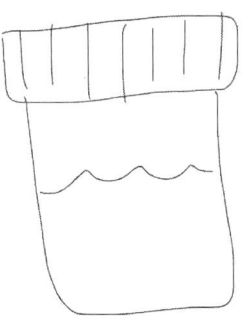

<u>waste.</u>
I'm tired of being wasted
wasting my time
on someone who's wasteful

<u>fragile.</u>
I wanted you to treat me
like I was your vape
when really
my heart was drywall
and your fist
was still your fist

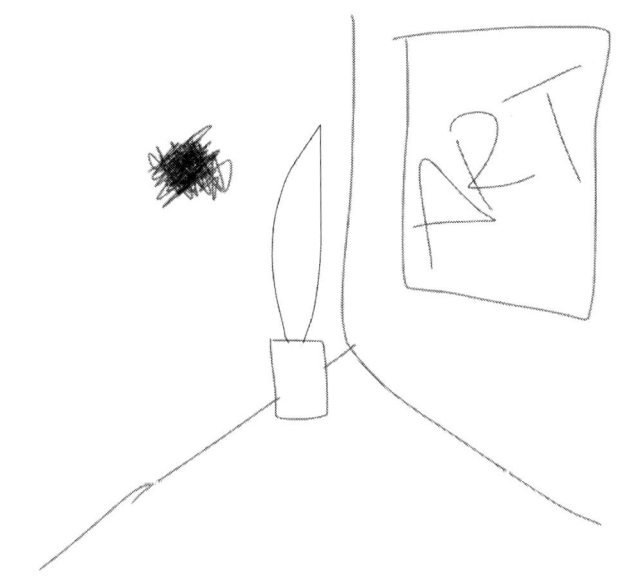

<u>sickly.</u>
my ash tray is empty
but I'm still full of cancer
because
I forgot sunscreen
and bathed in your
summer flame

<u>productive.</u>
I sat down
to finish my application
for school
and ended up watching
Twilight farts
on youtube instead

<u>you're welcome.</u>
being my friend is cool
because i either care about you
endlessly
being supportive in every aspect
and if not
well
you might get your dick wet
from time to time
which is also cool

and either way
you get to use me

mood.
sitting alone
in your car
in a dominoes parking lot
downtown
crying
and listening to
she will be loved
by maroon 5
at 1:00pm
on a saturday afternoon

<u>unimportant.</u>
the only person i talk to is myself
and even i
don't care

<u>issues.</u>
someone fall in love
with me
I probably won't reciprocate
but I'll still appreciate
your emotions for me

<u>stuck.</u>
again i sit
alone
staring outside
to the beautiful world
unable to gather the ability
to enjoy it
unable to lift myself
off the couch and out the door
unable to walk across the barrier
between me and freedom

i have no limbs

<u>complex.</u>
I've been scared of the dark
since I was a kid
I always thought I'd grow out of it
but now I'm 21 years old
and I still sleep with the lights on

hah.
sex with the devil
would be so hot

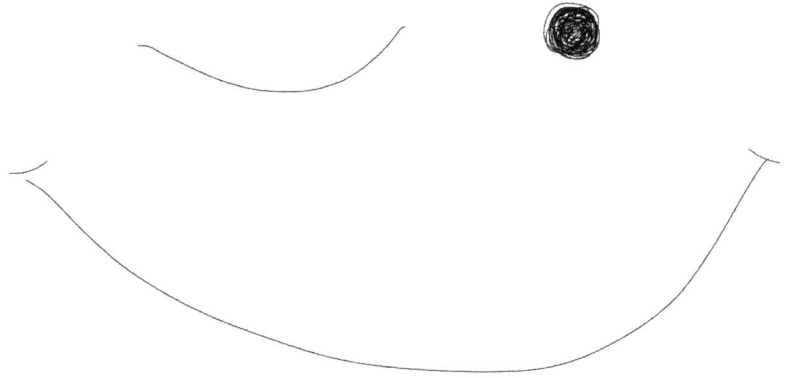

<u>sad.</u>
You asked me
if you could send me a dick pic
I said no
you pleaded
and pried
pathetically

      I have a question

Do you always
like to beg
like a little
  bitch
pig

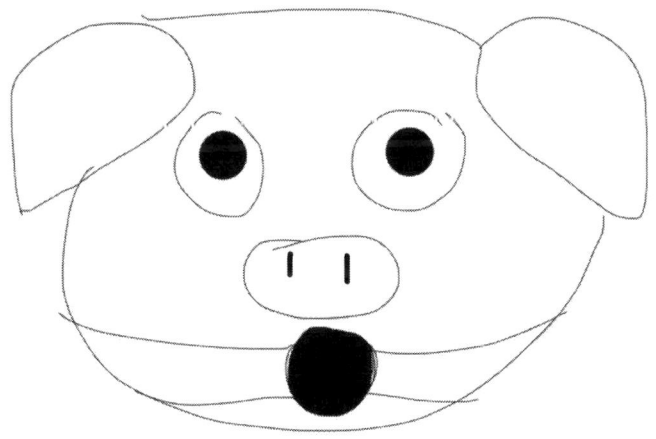

i'm (not) okay.
thorns
and thistles
and scratches on my arms
without any relation
toxicity and cancer
from casual
smoke inhalation

<u>wounded.</u>
scraped knees
don't bleed
when you have bandages
but i didn't
so i bled out

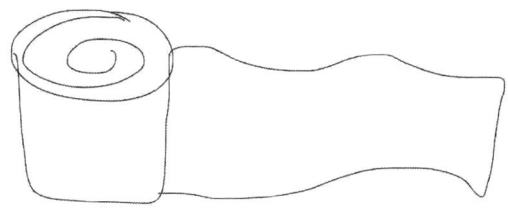

<u>path less travelled.</u>
My friends and I have a group-chat
where we keep track of local engagements
because there's been so many

All these people
having their life partners
in love
and then theres me
with (as of rn) 128 poems
that I wrote while high
shitting on other people

Different paths
I guess

<u>not shaming.</u>
I've never understood

humiliation kinks

I already humiliate myself enough.

don't really need anyone else's help

<u>disappointed.</u>
Kinky sex
doesn't just mean
  slamming
    my
      cervix,
              Chad.

don't push my fucking button

<u>pondering.</u>
If I go to the mall
on a busy day
how many babies
do you think i could
	punt
like a football
before security
catches me

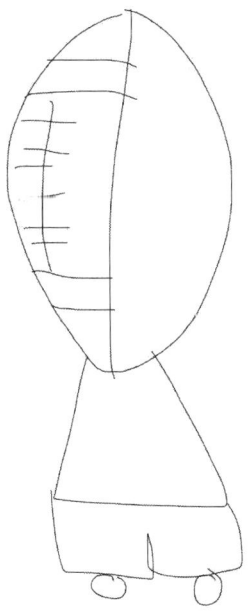

<u>time warp.</u>
I'm baked
at 10 am
on a thursday
about to make
KD for breakfast

I have regressed
into a teenage boy

<u>unfortunate.</u>
everyone that hates
the flavour
grape

is a

      mouth-breather

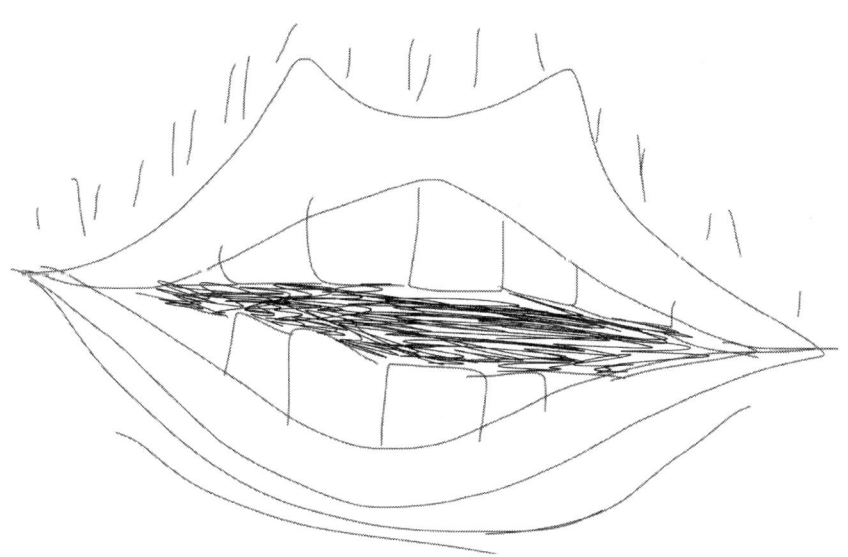

<u>screaming.</u>
I spoke into the microphone
but no sound came out
you unplugged the speaker
so no one could hear
what i had to say
unless i yelled
but you knew i had anxiety
and couldn't yell in crowds
so I was left
speechless

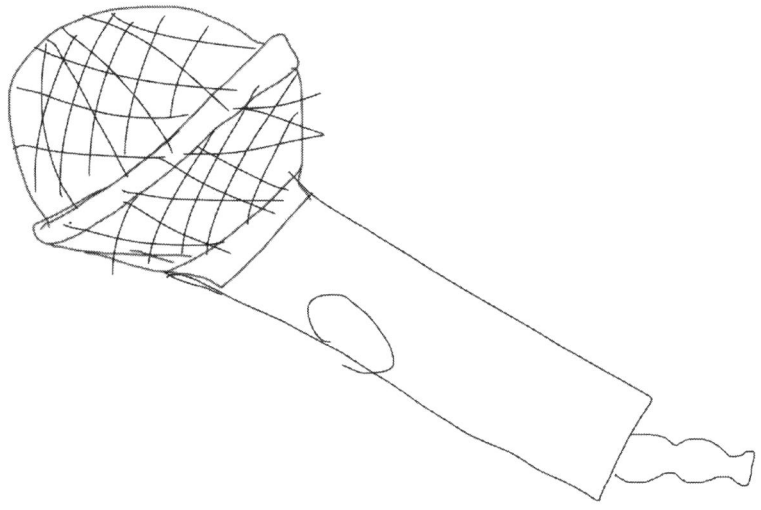

<u>why i'll never be classy.</u>
I never realized my family was white trash, until I reflected on a couple things:
  1. We never had winter gloves, so we'd just wear 2-3 pairs of old socks on our hands
  2. We waited for rainstorms to flood our cul-de-sac and pretended it was a pool
  3. Honestly the first two should be enough

<u>bruh.</u>
I'm so glad y'all love your bros so much
because u love them
ur bros
can u start actually holding them accountable
when they emotionally
and physically
abuse every single one of their partners
yknow
for the bros

<u>talentless.</u>
when using the word "you"
A lot of people don't know what to do
they're often so lazy, they rhyme it with another "you"
which is a silly, uninspired thing to do

the poëmless poem.

#igpoet.
your silence screams
like white noise
all i can hear is nothing
and everything
you ever said

<u>trash.</u>
what if the moon is a woman
and the stars are her babies
and the sun is an ain't shit father

<u>cringe past writing 4: middle school romance.(13)</u>
I see you
And my heart smiles
Baby just hold me for a while
Closing my eyes, I see you there
Open them, if I dare

You are my heart
My armour
My strength
My eyes glisten in the light
In which you bring, upon my life

I cannot sleep
You are all I see
I could never of guessed
The feelings would run this deep
Jealousy tears me apart
Watching her, enter your heart

I am blessed to know you,
Grateful to be close to you
But hateful to call you "friend"

<u>edgy.</u>
i burn myself with lighters
i want their flames to make me brighter

priorities.
dead eyes
but at least my brows are nice

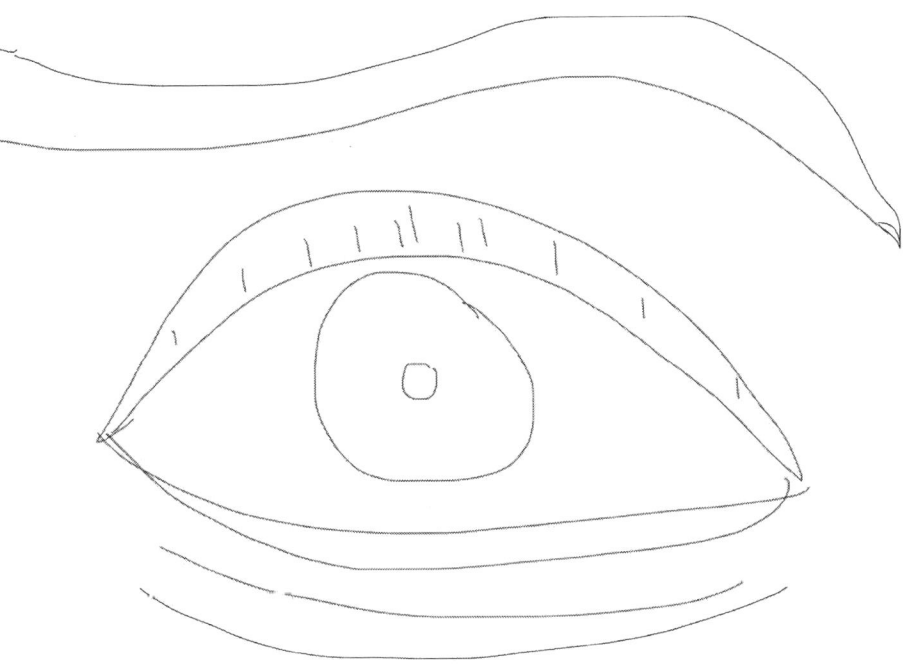

<u>look it up if you don't know, it's gnarly and you're dead.</u>
bitch
i stg
if you push me
i'll do to you
what king kong
did to the t-rex
in the movie
king kong

<u>clearly this couple should break up.</u>
vapid kisses
and vacant memories
rose petal poison
razor blade love
you
and
me

<u>uncomfortable.</u>
I'm not asking for a lot
I'm not looking for a california king
with a high thread count
sheet set
but you just have a single twin mattress on the floor
with no sheets, a torn comforter
and a discoloured pillow

I need something with a little more
support than that

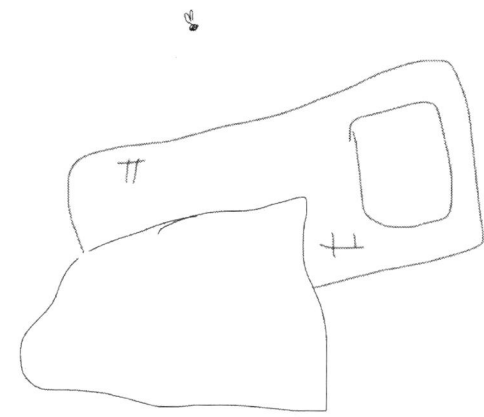

<u>copyright infringement.</u>
I'm all outta vape
I'm so lost with juuls

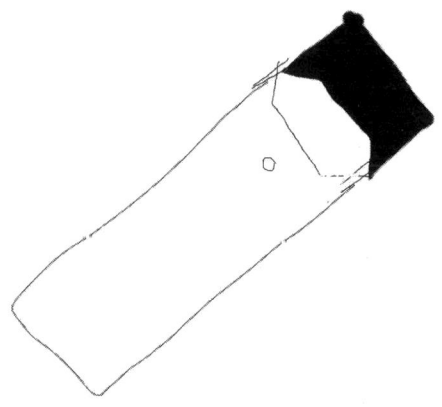

<u>home sweet home.</u>
small town locals be like
ah
love the smell of manure
and racism in the morning

<u>the nicest thing anyone's ever done for me.</u>
i was tripping hella
on psilocybin mushrooms
and i psyched myself out
thinking i saw liam neeson
in the streaks of the mirror in the room
so i called my best friend
and he came over
and cleaned the mirror for me

<u>chemical vs hormonal imbalance.</u>
am i feeling this way
because i'm having a mental health relapse
or am i just pmsing
i may
never know

<u>backwards.</u>
i almost hit someone with my car
because i was driving while crying
and I could hardly see through my tears
that's so wack
my depression is supposed to work on killing me
not strangers

<u>affection.</u>
I slap my ass often
self love

<u>text me when you see this one but also prepare yourself because there's another one coming up about you and it's worse than this one.</u>
I once knew a boy who said
giving someone a thumbs down
was worse than the middle finger
if you truly want to shame them

        Then, down the road,
        he acted like garbage
        so to communicate my disappointment
        I drew him as a thumbs down

proving yet again, women really do turn everything you say into a weapon

skidmark.
I hope kent state poop girl
can't find a toilet today

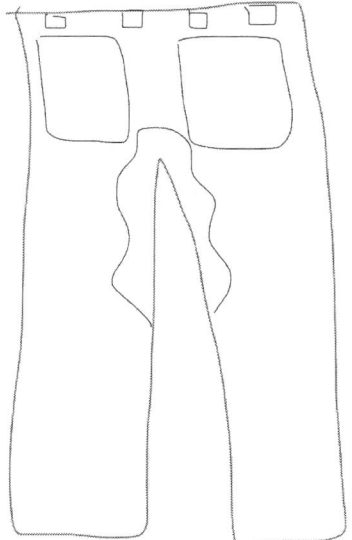

sludge.
There was a baby on the bus today
and it dead ass
looks like a sad fish

seriously
just look up
"ugly sea creature"
and it's the)c8 looking one

That is 100% what it looks like

I'm not wrong.

This is a funny joke and you can't make me feel bad.

cold.
you were a windstorm
and I forgot my jacket

<u>be a good citizen.</u>
not wiping snow
off your vehicle
before driving
is like not getting therapy
before dating new people

it's all going to collapse around you
which is not only dangerous for you
but those close to you

<u>don't recommend this actually.</u>
a little over a year ago
I was getting death threats in my voicemail
and instead of doing anything
I just didn't tell a single person
and eventually it stopped

moral of the story:
avoid your problems.

<u>dior.</u>

cigarettes
                             smoke
        lust   inhale
                                                                         cigarettes
scents   sex
                  golden aesthetic   flames
cigarettes
                                                                                           random
spin
                curtain flowing
                                            expensive jewelry
fragrance
                alluding to sex
sex
                                    cigarettes

<u>like prime rib or some shit even though I don't even like prime rib.</u>
I high key want to be taken on an expensive
and fancy ass date
one i gotta buy an entirely new
hot ass outfit for n shit
one where it would be rude
 to not put out at the end
yknow?
        FANCY.

<u>bring it.</u>
I'm so suicidal
I welcome being put in a saw trap
I wanna play a game, too
it's called
        kill me
bitch

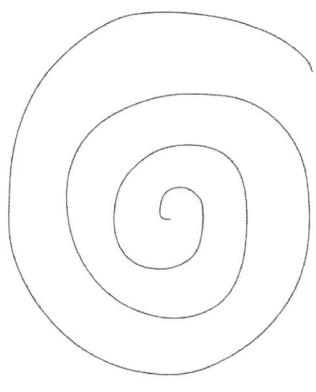

flaws.
the thing i hate most about myself
is that ill come home from a night of drinking
and think to myself
"yknow would make this night end on a good note?
if i kept taking shots before bed"

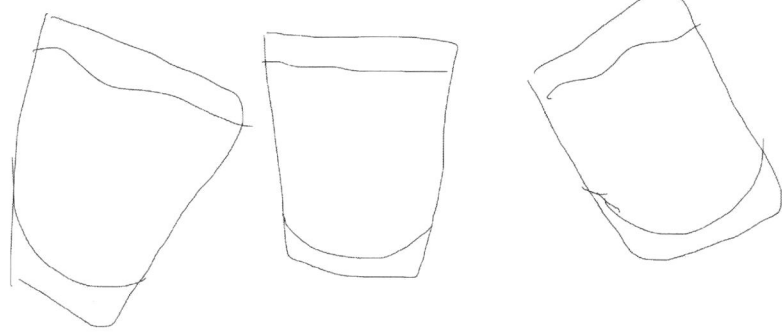

I'm too poor to shop leave me be.
I found photos of me from the seventh grade
wearing a band t-shirt
that I still own and wear regularly
nearly ten years later
my take?
glad I still have the awkward body of a middle school girl
with the style of a middle school boy

<u>terror.</u>
middle schoolers
are the scariest creatures on the planet.
they're terrifying, always
no matter your age

they are ruthless
they have no empathy
and they know
oh they know
that you can't him them

they scare younger kids by being mean
they scare us
by being fearless

<u>hurts.</u>
maybe nobody wants you
because you fucking reek
of desperation
you clingy
unloveable
overly sensitive
fuck
xoxo

<u>rip little foots mom.</u>
the animal I most resonate with
is a t-rex
because of my absolute unit of a head
and unfortunately stubby arms
also
and probably most relevant

I like to orphan children

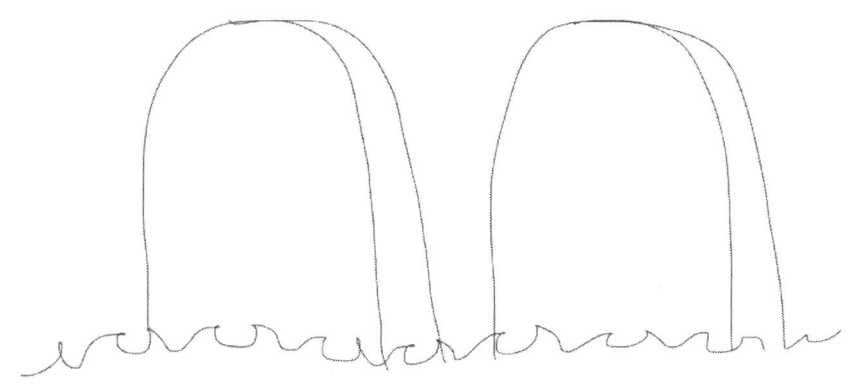

<u>call out type beat.</u>
never told anyone this
because it's fucking sad
but when i was in grade 10
i made a weird friend in my drama class
a grade 12 named sam

one day
a girl was singing in front of the class
and i said to sam "she's really beautiful"
to which he replied "oh yeah 10/10"

and then he looked at me
then back at her
and said
"you're about a 6"

uh

what
        the
                fuck
sam

didn't really ask?

<u>but actually if you hate it please don't tell me i can't handle criticism.</u>
the best part about this book
is that it can't be critiqued
it's too meta

"all of the poems were the same"
"they were all unoriginal"
that's the point, my guy

"not a single one was funny"
hurts,
but art is subjective so I forgive you

<u>ouch.</u>
Like a needle
hiding in a downtown park
you found your way
under my skin
and now I'm infected
with you

<u>Cringe past writing 5: feel inspired yet, bitch? (12)</u>
We all have the ability and capacity to overcome obstacles, but we lack the courage to try. One cannot simply breathe and do it, even though they can. It is not the disadvantage of physical disability; all is weighing down on mental capability. We miss and we miss with no try or swing, and everything in between are the words saying "you can't."

So look beyond that. Look beyond the failures, misses and the discouraged, run passed the broken and beaten creating your undestined destiny, and reach the land of the living. It's what we were made to do, and we can do it. All it takes is a try.

Failure is an illusion, fighting is the game, and living is the prize.

choking.
I was a confident smoker
until I took a toke of you

I haven't been able to breathe since

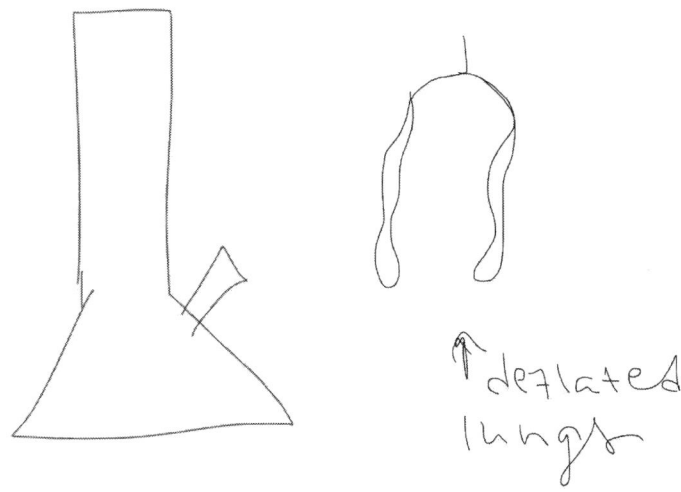

<u>incarcerated love.</u>
I am a dove
locked in a cage
set to be released
for a wedding
that never happened

goodbye.
I pray when you leave me
you part me with a kiss
A smooch would be nice
but also the chocolate though

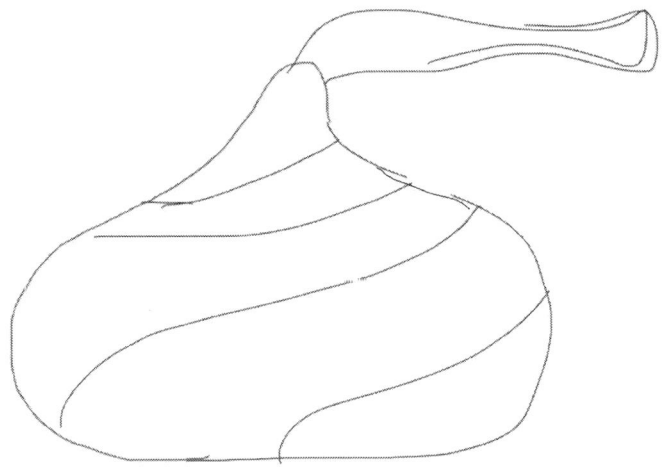

<u>self inflicted.</u>
It was sweater weather
but I wore a tee
I wanted to feel the bitter
like I did when you love me

<u>empty handed.</u>
waiting for you
is like waiting for christmas morning
when you know santa doesn't exist
and your family is poor

      it's depressing.

<u>eat it.</u>
ha ha
this ones for all the haters
who called me a psychopath
for leaving my bedroom window open
24/7 during winter:
uh it's frozen over and stuck
so i couldn't shut it now
even if i wanted to

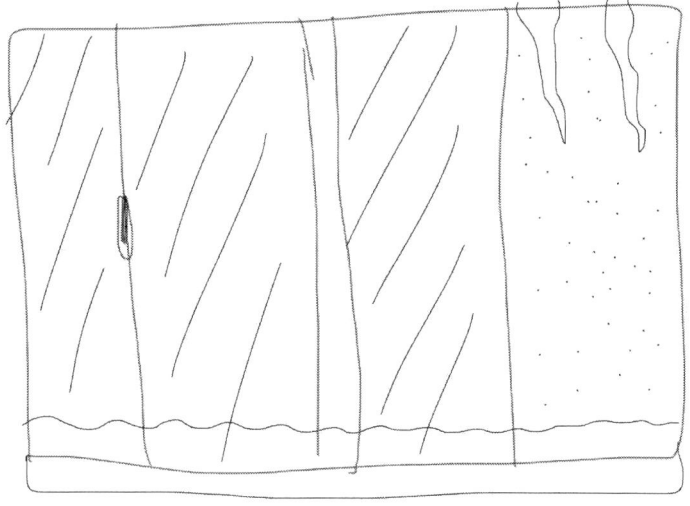

<u>i'm not even sorry.</u>
don't date me
and certainly don't break my heart
because i will be butt hurt
and i will write
an entire book of poetry about you

Things that we don't fuck with.
  1. Rapists
  2. Supporting rapists
  3. Not calling out rapists
  4. Not supporting victims

24 hour rape crisis & info line: 604 255 6344

<u>broken closet doors.</u>
I don't think I've ever
really been open with my extended family
about my sexuality
so here it is

<u>self involved.</u>
I tried
I tried to get you to care
to notice
to help
but I was just a check-engine light
and you were a twenty-something white girl

<u>caged.</u>
barbed wire fences
surrounding my heart
I'll never trust again
since our love tore apart
I whispered a name once
and it screamed louder than sin
so I'll never speak again
with my blood frozen within

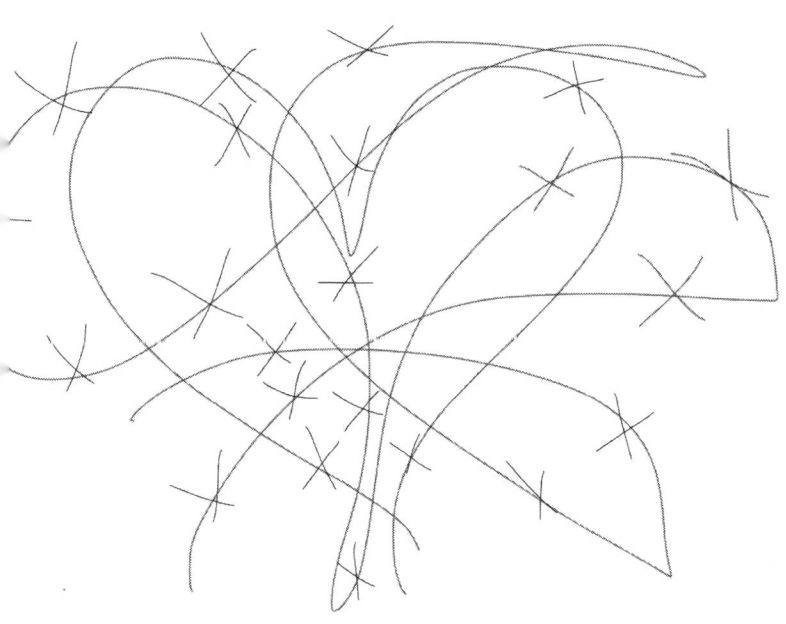

<u>edge queen.</u>
if I smoked more would i be enough
if I died more would you want me
i'm thinking of ways to make my blood more toxic
so one day you might love me

<u>sweaty.</u>
summers heat
dries out
my heart
on my sleeve

<u>society.</u>
girls always get shit on
for breaking up with
or not picking
"nice guys"
but men are never called out
for abusing
nice girls

<u>i just wanted to compliment your makeup.</u>
do you ever waste
your drunk girl bathroom niceness
on a really rude girl
and you're left feeling like you're back in high school
sitting under the stairs at lunch
too anxious to walk the halls

and it just
it hurts all over again

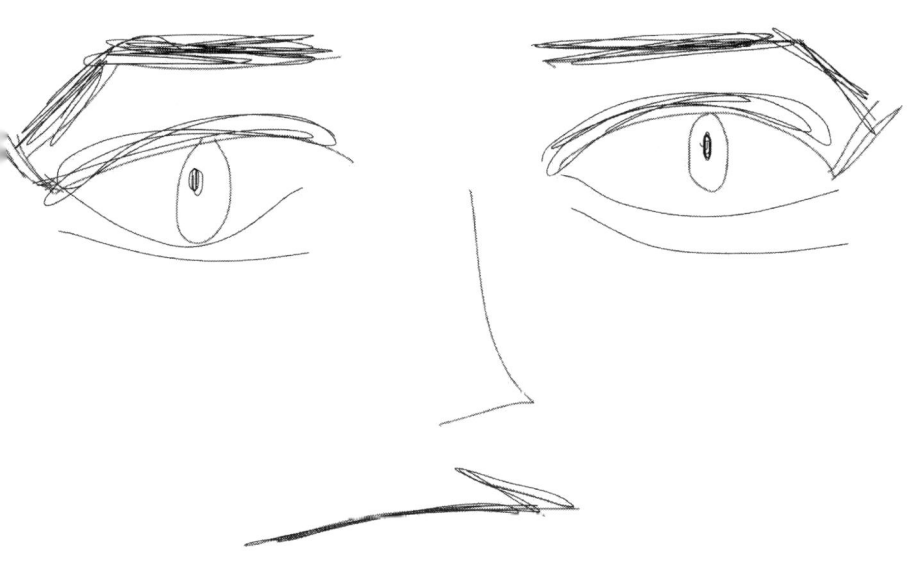

<u>why.</u>
my dad has never sneezed
quieter than a murder scream

<u>metaphor.</u>
I broke my built in retainer
by eating my chicky nuggies too aggressively
and now it cuts my tongue
whenever I move it

I never did know
how to enjoy the good
without also suffering in the bad

<u>tumblr 4.0</u>
jaded remains
love
in vain
i'm always in pain
minds gone insane
      cigarettes

<u>spoof.</u>
I just accidentally deleted ten new poems
and tried to recover them
but didn't know how
so I pressed the trash can button again
hoping it would possibly "undelete" them
therein completely erasing them
altogether

idk I just think there's a metaphor in there somewhere

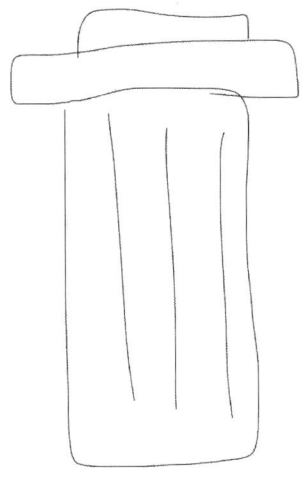

vigilante.
sometimes I think about
the amount of lives I've probably saved
by using a condom
instead of the letting the guy finish inside me
therein creating the worlds most psychopathic infant

I don't want to say this makes me batman
but I'm definitely batman

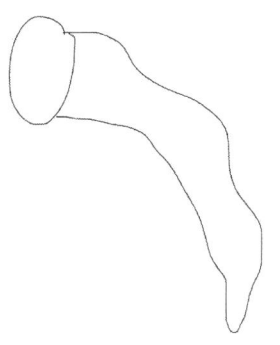

relatable.
having depression is like being a track runner
but your leg keeps falling off
but everyone still expects you to do well
and run as fast as everyone else
as if your entire ass limb isn't just
detaching???
from your body

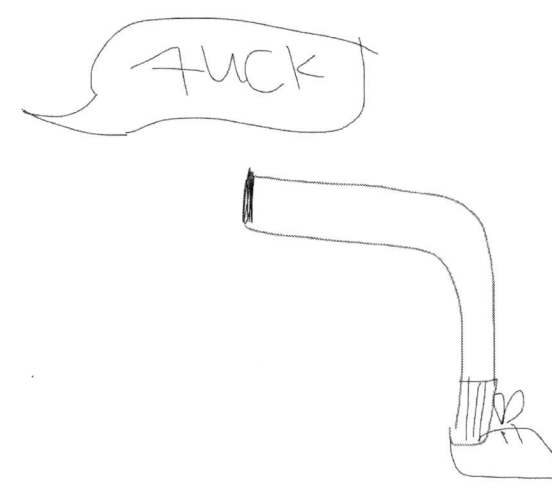

Cringe past writing 6: deep thoughts for a 12 year old (12)

Darkness. It fills the air and everything around me. Everywhere I look, it seems to be compelled with rage or sorrow. Is there nothing that can truly be 'happy'? Along with lies and tears there is shame and fear. Is there any way to escape this? Is there are world beyond ours that we can truly call home? A world entirely our own, not only in our dreams but simply beyond our reach? Is it that all we need to do is forget the rage or sorrow, and the same and fear, and just live

rekt,
you told me to kill myself
because no one would care
well jokes on you, guy
because the voices in my head would
and that's 10 people at least

<u>uninvited.</u>
why did the internet make it seem
like every teenager was out
getting drunk on rooftops

yknow how left out i felt
because i couldn't get on my roof

it's misleading

i'm joking, kink shaming is wrong.
i'm pretty fucked up
and i like pretty
questionable
sex acts
but at least i don't have
a foot fetish

<u>secrets.</u>
I could never be famous
I'm too scared of what people might dig up on me
like
how my ass is so fat
or that I'm too giving in bed
or that I breed my dog
just so I can drown the puppies

recent google searches.
Common ways of suicide
How long to die from breathing in car fumes
How long to die from hanging
How to tie a noose
How much is rope
How long to die from bleeding out
Main arteries
Carotid arteries
Blood thinners
Techno seals video

24/7 suicide helpline: text HELLO to 686868

redundant.
I tried to run away from my problems
but I was on a treadmill

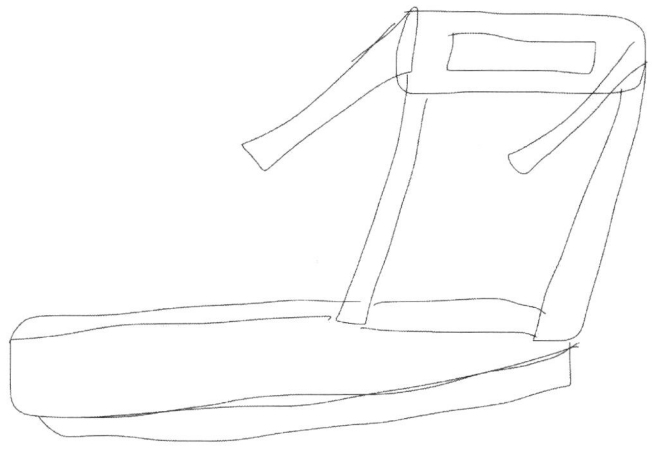

<u>my moms horse painting.</u>
you lurk in the shadows
with a sinister smirk
painted subtly across your face
and stand with a predator stance
waiting to strike

<u>i'm not wrong.</u>
old people shouldn't drive.

<u>yummy.</u>
Your cigarette ash
danced in the air
and I let it fall on my tongue
like a snowflake in winter

I was always so willing
to glorify your poison

<u>hahahaha.</u>
I'm whipping out these poems
faster than your dad
whips out his dick for me

<u>hope you find a diet that works.</u>
When I worked at a gas station
some middle schoolers were trying
to get people to boot them smokes
so I kicked them off the property
Clearly they did not agree with my decision
because one yelled out to me
"Suck my fat cock"

Uh

:/
Bro sorry your penis is obese

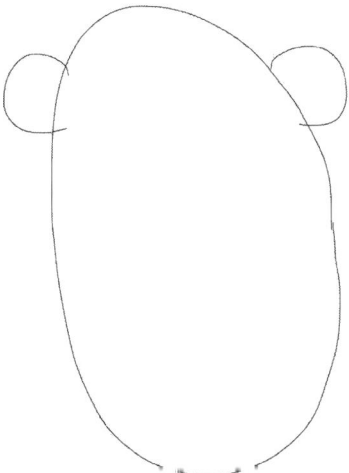

endless.
I drove so fast
down your highway of manipulation
I didn't notice
it had no off ramps

<u>lel.</u>
I promise
no matter what type of poetry I'm writing
whether it's satirical or honest
I will never half ass it
I will always put the utmost

<u>caw.</u>
Yesterday I saw a crow
(something I used to think was beautiful)
trying to kill an innocent squirrel,
that ran for its life in horror.
Now I worry
about the murder
inside of me

<u>rip.</u>
I'm only in my early twenties
and I've already taken
four sabbaticals off work
due to stress
I can't wait
for the next 60 years

<u>boom.</u>
my sister loves the meme
        it really do be like that sometimes
except she's 27
and so she tries
but she often says a variation of

it really is that way sometimes
sometimes it really is that way
it's really like that some days

she tries

<u>it's a joke don't come @ me.</u>
hey
hot take:
just because you hit
        enter
in the middle
of your sentences
doesn't mean you know
how to write a poem

<u>bet.</u>
that message may have been sappy
but i am not weak
and i will still scrap a motherfucker

<u>the worst first kiss ever.</u>
I ate some bad breakfast
from a restaurant I normally enjoy
and it made it not so pleasant
when I hung out with a very cute boy
He leaned in to kiss me
just as my stomach because to feel nauseous
I had to rush away quickly
because I was beginning to projectile vomit
I made it to the toilet
my stomach a triggered nuke
afterwards he laughed at me,
but that's okay, because he will always be the boy
who's kiss made me puke

change.
I rolled you a joint
you said you'd upgraded to dabs

<u>illness.</u>
I feel sick
and I can't tell
if it's because I'm so hungry
or if I'm actually sick

that's the hard part about destruction
you never know if you're the cause
or if it's just engrained inside of you

a contrast this obvious isn't poetry (this is direct shade at my own writing).
i am frozen
next to the sun

<u>hmmm.</u>
maybe
zack
no girl has ever been able to
"deep throat your cock"
because you don't have a cock
big enough
to deep throat

<u>full.</u>
I swallowed my feelings
filling up
on sadness rather than sustenance
thank you
I'm skinny now

<u>empty.</u>
you make my eyes pee
I wish my heart
had a bigger bladder

(this was supposed to be a bladder)

<u>maybe one day.</u>
my personality rn
is just baked
I'm stoned all the time
but it's either this
or suicidal
and what would you prefer?

therapy probably.

Manufactured by Amazon.ca
Bolton, ON